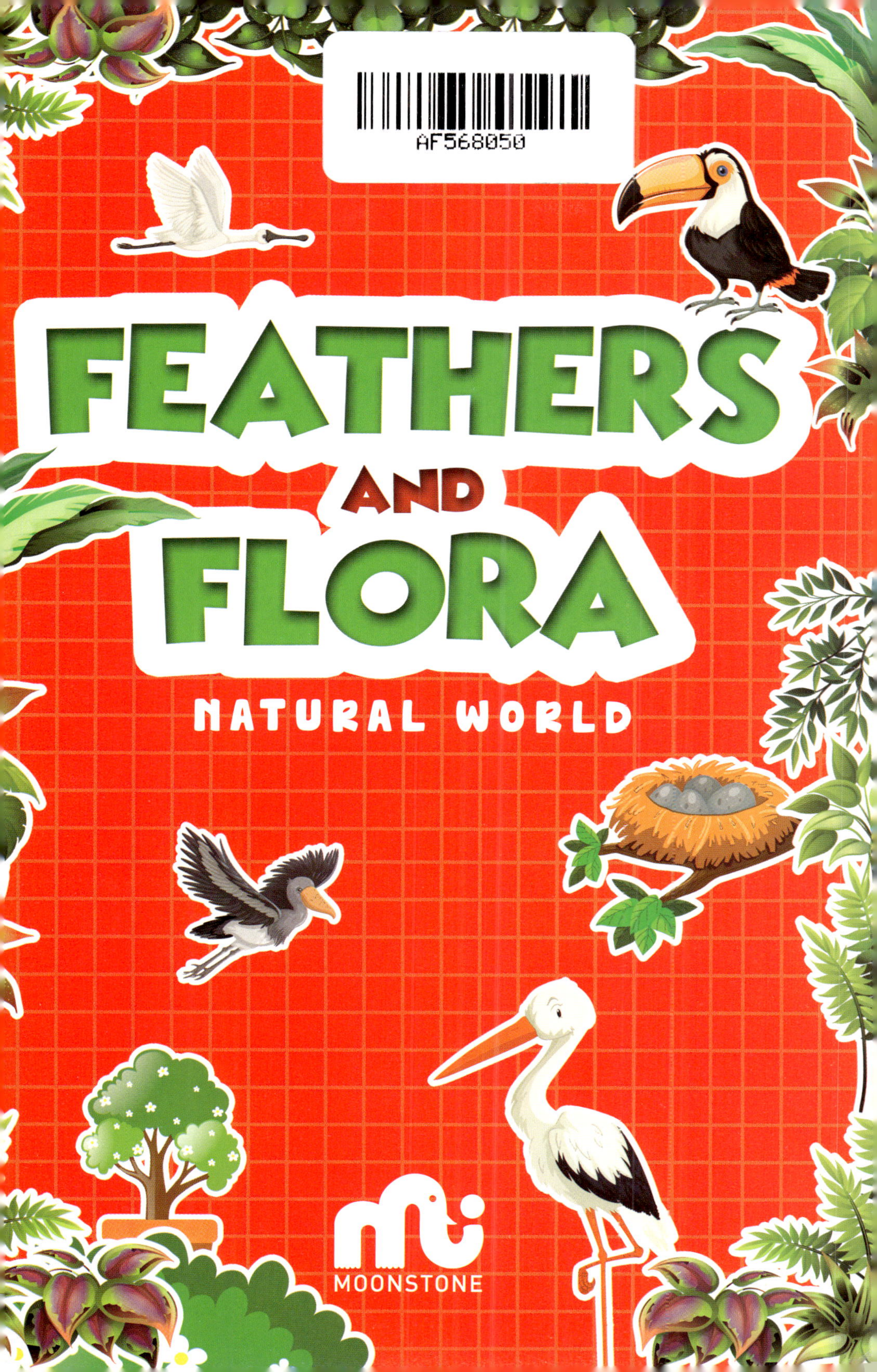
AF568050
FEATHERS
AND
FLORA
NATURAL WORLD
MOONSTONE

Published in Moonstone
by Rupa Publications India Pvt. Ltd 2024
7/16, Ansari Road, Daryaganj
New Delhi 110002

Sales centres:
Bengaluru Chennai
Hyderabad Jaipur Kathmandu
Kolkata Mumbai Prayagraj

P-ISBN: 978-93-5702-439-6
E-ISBN: 978-93-5702-429-7

First impression 2024

10 9 8 7 6 5 4 3 2 1

Printed in India

CONTENTS

BIRDS

Introduction 6
Ancient Birds 8
Flightless Birds 10
Perching Birds 12
Birds of Prey 14
Falcons 16
Owls 18
Freshwater Birds and Shorebirds 20
Seabirds 22
Gulls 24
Migratory Birds 26
Rainforest Birds 28
Pigeons and Doves 30
Building Nests 32
Eggs and Babies 34
Birds as Pets 36
The Champions 38
Endangered Birds 40
Extinct Birds 42
Glossary 44
Answers 46

CONTENTS

PLANTS

Introduction 48

Trees 50

Parts of a Plant 52

Photosynthesis 54

Flowering and Non-Flowering 56

Parts of a Flower 58

Pollination 60

Germination 62

Shrub 64

Grass 66

Vine 68

Conifer 70

Fern 72

Moss 74

Aquatic Plants 76

Desert Plants 78

Medicinal Plants 80

Carnivorous Plants 82

Botanical Gardens 84

Glossary 86

Answers 88

NATURAL WORLD
BIRDS

Introduction

Birds are unique because they can fly. They are the only animals that have feathers. Feathers keep a bird's body warm and help it to fly. The colourful feathers and musical songs of birds have made them one of the most loved animals.

Some birds are known for their ability to fly thousands of miles from one continent to another, while others make popular pets. There are more than 10,000 species of birds in the world, ranging from tiny hummingbirds to large condors. Birds of various sizes inhabit every corner of the world.

Ancient Birds

The first birds appeared around 150 million years ago. Scientists believe that birds evolved from small meat-eating dinosaurs.

Archaeopteryx

Archaeopteryx is the oldest known bird. It had characteristics of both reptiles and birds. It had claws like reptiles and teeth and feathers like birds. Fossils of Archaeopteryx were dug up from a swamp in Germany in 1861.

- Stirton's Thunderbird weighed up to 500 kilograms (1100 pounds).
- Archaeopteryx walked like a bird, even though it had claws like a reptile.

Rahonavis

Rahonavis was a bird-like dinosaur that lived about 70 million years ago on the island of Madagascar. It was almost the size of a raven and was more bird-like than the archaeopteryx.

Stirton's Thunderbird

Stirton's Thunderbird was a huge flightless bird that lived 8 million years ago in Australia. Fossils of this species of bird have been found in the Northern Territory of Australia.

Name the oldest known bird.

Flightless Birds

Birds are known for their ability to fly, but there are many birds that cannot fly. Such birds usually live in isolated areas or islands where they do not have many predators. Flightless birds have wings, but their wings only protect them from heat and cold and help them maintain their balance while running.

Ostrich

The ostrich is the largest and the heaviest bird alive. It is a tall bird with long, powerful legs, making it a fast runner. It can run up to 70 kilometers (43.5 miles) an hour. The ostrich lives in the open grasslands of Africa.

Emu

The Emu is a tall, flightless bird found commonly in the woodlands of Australia. It is the largest bird in Australia and the second-largest in the world. The emu has small wings and a long neck. They are fast runners, like ostriches.

Rhea

The rhea is a large, flightless bird found in South America. There are two groups of rhea—Greater rhea and Darwin's rhea. The greater rhea is found in the eastern parts of South America,, while Darwin's rhea is found in Altiplano and Patagonia, in South America.

- Ostriches have the largest eyes of any land animal.
- Emus lay emerald-green or dark green eggs.
- The weight of an ostrich egg is equivalent to the weight of about 24 chicken eggs.

Kiwi

The kiwi is a small, flightless bird. It is about 30 centimetres (about 12 inches) tall and is covered with rough, brown feathers. Kiwis have a long, pointed bill, with nostrils at the end. They use it to sniff out bugs to eat.

? **Which is the largest and heaviest bird alive?**

Perching Birds

Perching birds are the most common type of bird. There are over 5,000 identified species of perching birds. One of the most important physical features of these birds is their grasping feet, which help them hold and perch on tree branches.

Songbird

Songbirds are small, perching birds that sing melodious, musical songs. Common songbirds include warblers, wrens, bulbuls, swallows, nightingales, cuckoos, orioles, and finches.

Finch

Finches are small, seed-eating birds. There are about 240 kinds of finches in the world. Common finches include canaries, yellow finches, warbling finches, house finches, zebra finches, etc.

Swallows

Swallows are small, swift fliers with long, pointed wings. They spend most of their time flying. They are known for their ability to feed themselves while flying. They hunt insects such as flies, mosquitoes, and gnats.

Bulbul

Bulbuls are medium-sized songbirds found in Africa and Asia. Most bulbuls are grey or black, with red, yellow, or orange markings. Some may also have a crest on their head.

- Lyrebirds are songbirds that can mimic any sound.
- Ravens are the largest perching birds.
- Pipits and larks are songbirds that sing while in flight.

? How many kinds of finches are there in the world?

Birds of Prey

Some birds are great hunters. They are known as birds of prey, or raptors. These birds hunt animals and may even scavenge on dead animals. Most raptors are larger than other birds. They have sharp talons and hooked beaks, which they use to hunt and to cut and tear their prey.

Vulture

Vultures are birds of prey that feed on dead or weak animals. They have broad, powerful wings that help them soar high up in the sky. They have slow wing beats, and flap their wings once per second.

Eagle

Eagles are large, powerful birds of prey. The golden eagle, a common species of eagle, hunts mice, rats, rabbits, birds, and reptiles. The bald eagle, which lives close to lakes and rivers, eats fish and birds. Some eagles feed on dead animals too.

Hawk

Hawks and eagles belong to the hawk family. However, hawks are smaller than eagles. All hawks have strong beaks and powerful vision.

- Vultures can digest bones.
- Eagles can dive at a speed of about 240 kilometers (about 150 miles) per hour.
- The bald eagle is the national symbol of the United States of America.

? Which bird is the national symbol of the United States of America?

Falcons

Falcons are birds of prey that have long, pointed wings and are characterised by their swift, fast, and strong flight. There are nearly 40 species of falcons, which are spread in areas of Europe, Asia, and North America. They usually nest in holes in trees or on natural shelves on cliffs.

Kestrels

Kestrels are distinctive-looking, small, stocky falcons that have bright feathers. They are 13–15 inches long and have a 26–32-inch wingspan. Males are more beautiful than females, with a chestnut brown back and bluish-grey head and wings. However, female kestrels are larger than males. Kestrels feed on insects, small mammals, rodents, and birds.

- Kestrels do not build their own nest; they use nests made by other birds.
- During the mid-20th century, peregrine falcons were almost wiped out of eastern North America due to pesticide poisoning.

Peregrine

Peregrines are among the world's most common birds of prey. They are found on all continents except Antarctica. They are powerful and fast falcons that hunt medium-sized birds.

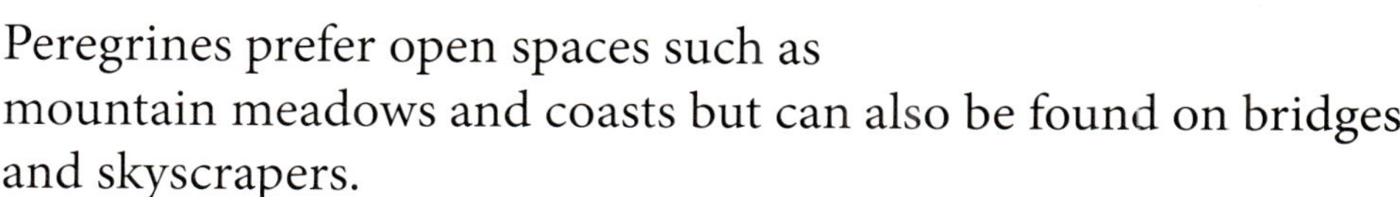

Peregrines prefer open spaces such as mountain meadows and coasts but can also be found on bridges and skyscrapers.

Hobbies

Hobbies are slightly larger and more elegant falcons. They have a dark slate-grey plumage and a black malar region. They are fast flyers and have pointed wings. They hunt birds and large insects such as dragonflies.

? Male kestrels are larger than female kestrels. (True or false)

Owls

Owls are raptors and have a sharp beak and pointed claws. They are mostly nocturnal creatures and prefer to live a solitary life. There are around 250 species of owls, which are found throughout the world except Antarctica.

Predators

Owls are silent hunters of the night. They mostly feed on small mammals like mice, squirrels, and rabbits. Owls do not have teeth. They do not chew their food but swallow it completely, including the skin, bones, and feathers. However, they later regurgitate the undigested food.

Facts

- There are 16 living species of barn owl.
- The smallest owl, Elf owl that is six inches (15 centimeters) in height is hundred times smaller than the largest owl, Eurasian Eagle Owl.
- Only short eared owls and snowy owls are day time hunters, rest are active at night.

Barn Owls

Barn owls belong to the family ***Tytonidae***. They are medium-to large-sized birds that have large heads, long legs, and powerful talons. Barn owls have heart-shaped faces made up of stiff feathers, which help them locate the source of sounds. They are usually orange-brown in colour, with the back being slightly darker.

Typical Owls

True owls, or typical owls, belong to the family Strigidae. They are much more diverse than barn owls. They have round facial discs, large heads, and short tails. Their wings are large, rounded, and soft, with a downy base that allows them to fly silently. They are brown, rusty, grey, white, and black with a mottled pattern, which helps them in camouflage.

What is the shape of a barn owl's face?

Freshwater Birds and Shorebirds

Freshwater birds and shorebirds (wading birds) spend most of their time in and around bodies of water. They usually nest in trees or bushes near ponds, lakes, rivers, and seashores. Birds found around freshwater bodies include swans, ducks, kingfishers, moorhens, and grebes.

Crane

Cranes are tall wading birds found in almost all continents, except South America and Antarctica. They have long necks and bills, and big rounded wings. They usually feed on fish, insects and snakes.

Duck, Swan and Goose

Ducks, swans and geese are waterfowl that are found on all continents except Antarctica. They have waterproof wings, short legs and webbed feet, which help them float and swim in water.

Flamingo

Flamingos are large pink-to crimson-coloured wading birds. They have long, hooked beaks and long legs that help them wade deeper than any other bird. Flamingos eat algae, small water insects and crustaceans such as shrimp.

- The giant kingfisher is the largest species of kingfisher.
- The whooping crane is the tallest bird of North America.
- The sarus crane is the tallest flying bird in the world.

Anhinga

Anhingas (water turkeys or snakebirds) are large water birds. They have a long neck and a sharp-pointed bill. Unlike most water birds, anhingas do not have waterproof feathers. So often, after a swim, they perch on trees with open wings to dry their feathers and warm their bodies.

Common Kingfisher

Common kingfishers are small, brightly coloured birds with blue-green wings found in Europe, Africa, and Asia. They live around ponds, streams, lakes, and rivers. Kingfishers feed on aquatic insects and small fish. Once they see a fish in the water, they dive in and fly out with the fish in their beak.

What type of wings do swans have?

Seabirds

Freshwater birds and shorebirds (wading birds) spend most of their time in and around bodies of water. They usually nest in trees or bushes near ponds, lakes, rivers and seashores. Birds found around freshwater bodies include swans, ducks, kingfishers, moorhens and grebes.

Albatross

Albatross are the largest seabirds. They usually have a white-coloured body with long, narrow wings, short legs, and a short tail. Albatross spend most of their lives wandering above the Southern Ocean in Antarctica.

Penguin

Penguins are flightless birds that live in the coastal areas of the Southern Hemisphere.
There are 18 species of penguins. Penguins have webbed feet and paddle-like flippers that help them swim and dive in the water.

Tern

Terns (sea swallows) are common shorebirds. They have long pointed wings, a straight bill and a slender body. Terns feed on fish and insects found in the water.

Skua

Skuas are large seabirds with long and powerful hooked bills. They feed on fish and eggs of other birds. There are 7 species of skuas—the great skua, Arctic skua, pomarine skua, Chilean skua, south polar skua, brown skua, and long-tailed skua. The great skua is the largest skua.

- The regal Caspian Tern is the largest tern, and the Least Tern is the smallest tern.
- Emperor penguins, found in Antarctica, are the largest penguins.
- The Antarctic Tern is a small bird found throughout the Antarctic region.

How many species of penguins are there?

Gulls

Gulls are a familiar group of birds that are found throughout the world in coastal and inland habitats. They are often the largest birds found along the shore. There are above 50 species of gulls found throughout the world.

Physical Description

Gulls have long, narrow wings, long necks, and deep, broad chests. They have short tails and strong webbed feet with small talons. Their webbed feet allow them to walk as well to take off quickly from water.

Facts

- Gulls have 'salt glands', which make them capable of drinking both fresh water and salt water.
- Gulls can fly at great heights for long durations without flapping.
- Gulls nest in large, densely packed bird colonies.

Bill and Plumage

Gulls have heavy and stout, slightly hooked bills, which give them an advantage over a varied diet. They generally have markings such as coloured spots, coloured tips, or contrasting bands over them. Feathers of gulls are not typically colourful and are usually grey, white, or black in colour.

Food and Eating Habits

Gulls feed on fish, mollusks, insects, worms and rodents. They often find easy meals in trash cans and other discarded food items. They are also intelligent enough to find ways to steal food from other animals.

What type of feet do gulls have?

Migratory Birds

Migration is a natural process. Most birds migrate to different corners of the world at different times of the year in search of a warmer climate, food, and suitable breeding places. Some fly from north to south during the autumn to escape the cold winters of the north and fly back in the springtime.

Routes and Patterns

Migratory birds usually fly in flocks, forming different patterns in the sky. Birds such as ducks, geese and cranes form a V-shaped pattern in the sky, while some birds fly in slanting lines.

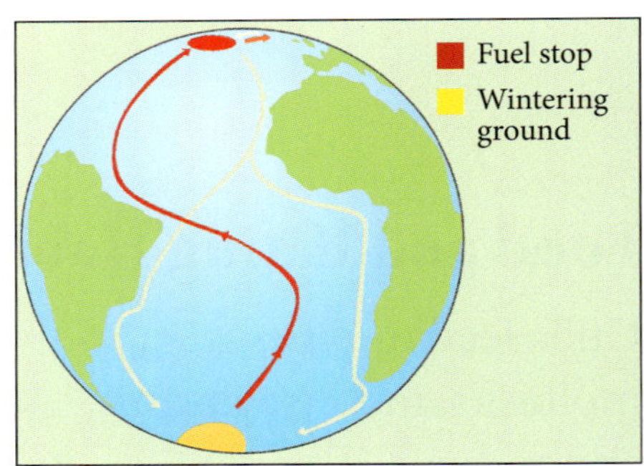

Preparing for the Journey

Migratory birds start preparing for their journey long before its onset. They fatten themselves up and replace their old feathers with new ones. Long trips require the feathers to be perfect. Once they are ready, they wait for the right weather conditions to begin their flight.

Arctic Tern

The Arctic Tern makes the longest journey of all birds. It nests and breeds in the Arctic and spends the winter season in the Antarctic. From the North Pole to the South Pole and then back, the Arctic Tern covers a distance of almost 90,000 km (55,923 miles) every year.

- Whooping cranes can migrate up to 800 kilometers (about 497 miles) in a day.
- Most migratory songbirds travel at night.
- Penguins migrate by swimming.

Bar-headed Geese

Bar-headed geese migrate from northern Asia to India and Burma in south Asia. On their long journey, they fly above the Himalayan range. They have been seen at heights higher than 6,540 metres (21,460 ft),, where oxygen is scarce and life is rare. These birds spend their winters in northeastern India, northern Burma and Pakistan and return to their nests in southeast Russia and western China in the spring.

Which bird migrates the longest distance?

Rainforest Birds

Rainforests are warm, dense evergreen forests that receive a lot of rainfall throughout the year. The rainforests of the Amazon and Indonesia are home to almost 50 percent of all birds in the world. Many bright and colourful birds also inhabit the rainforests of Australia.

Toucan

Toucans are brightly coloured birds found in the rainforests of South America. They have a short, rounded body and a large beak. In some species of toucans, the beaks are almost half the size of their bodies.

Facts

- The hyacinth macaw is the largest macaw and the red-shouldered macaw is the smallest macaw.
- Peacocks are big birds with long beautiful tails that are found in Asia and Africa.
- Lovebirds are small parrots found in the forests of Africa.

Macaw

Macaws are the largest members of the parrot family. They are covered with blue, red, yellow, or green-coloured feathers. They are found in the forests of South America, Central America, and Mexico.

Laughing Kookaburra

Laughing kookaburras are the largest members of the kingfisher family. They are found in the forests and open woodlands in Australia.

Which is the largest member of the parrot family?

Pigeons and Doves

Pigeons and doves belong to the same family. Pigeons are bigger than doves. There are over 350 species of pigeons and doves.

Mourning Dove

Mourning doves get their name from the sad cooing call they make. They are slate blue-coloured and are found in North America.

Facts

- Ancestors of the modern carrier pigeon used to carry messages from one place to another.
- Pigeons and doves are popular game birds.
- Ground doves are the smallest doves.

Habitat

From deserts and dense forests to urban areas, pigeons and doves inhabit almost all kinds of habitats. Many bird lovers keep pigeons and doves as pets.

Rock Pigeon

Rock pigeons are the most common pigeons. They usually nest in urban areas, agricultural areas and cliffsides. These pigeons feed on corn, grains and even bread.

How many species of pigeons and doves are there?

Building Nests

Birds build nests to lay eggs and raise their young. The nests protect the eggs and the nestlings from predators such as snakes, rodents and other birds. Different birds build different types of nests.

Simple Nest

Many shorebirds, terns, hawks, and vultures live in small depressions or among leaf litter and debris on the ground. Other forms of simple bird nests are flat, platform nests built on the ground or in shallow water. Another kind of simple nest is the common cup-shaped nest.

Tailorbird

Tailorbirds are small, brightly coloured birds found in Southeast Asia. These birds build funnel-shaped nests by piercing large, green leaves with their long, curved bills and sewing them together with plant fibre.

Tree Hollows

Tree hollows in the trunks and branches of old or dying trees serve as homes for many birds. Some birds, such as woodpeckers, hollow out their nests in tree trunks, while others such as owls and cockatoos live in existing, natural tree hollows.

Birds Without Nests

Some birds do not build any nest at all. Instead, they lay their eggs on the ground, in broken tree stumps, or on rocks or sand. For example, female emperor penguins lay their eggs on the ground while cuckoos lay their eggs in the nests of other birds.

Facts

- All flightless birds nest on the ground or in burrows.
- Some weaverbirds build apartment-like nests that have 100–300 chambers.
- The nests of some species of swiftlets are used as the main ingredients of bird's nest soupa Chinese delicacy.

? **Which bird builds a funnel shaped nest?**

Eggs and Babies

All female adult birds lay eggs. The babies develop inside the eggs, and when they are ready to hatch, they break out of the egg shell. The hard shell of the egg protects the baby growing inside it.

Eggs

Eggs of different birds vary in size, colour, and appearance. The egg provides food to the developing baby until it is born.

Incubation

Parents keep the egg warm after it is laid. This is called incubation. Incubation periods vary in different birds. For example, chickens take 20-22 days to hatch, while ostriches take 36-45 days.

Hatching

Chicks hatch after incubation. Most newly hatched chicks are blind and do not have feathers. However, babies of some birds like ducks, are born with open eyes and are covered with downy feathers.

Young Ones

Young ones of different species remain in the nest for different periods, and their parents take care of them.

Largest and Smallest Eggs

Ostriches lay the largest eggs of all birds, and bee hummingbirds lay the smallest eggs.

- A female kiwi can lay up to 100 eggs in her lifetime.
- The young ones of swans are called cygnets.
- Female hummingbirds usually lay two eggs at a time.

Which birds lay the smallest eggs?

Birds as Pets

Birds are popular pets. Most birds are kept as pets because they are beautiful and people enjoy their songs. Before buying a pet bird, it is very important to find out whether the bird is healthy or not. Birds that are not active and playful may be sick. Bright eyes, shiny feathers, and a good appetite ensure that the bird is healthy.

Cockatiel

Cockatiels are small parrots native to Australia. They make excellent pets. They have a long tail and a crest on their heads.

Food for Pet Birds

Birds love to eat seeds and nuts. In the wild, they feed on many fruits. Pet birds should be given a balanced diet of seeds, fruits and green vegetables. They should also be given a lot of fresh water to drink every day. Many pet birds even enjoy bits of chicken or hard-boiled eggs.

Canary

Canaries are small, colourful birds. They are one of the most popular songbirds. Male canaries usually sing better than females. Canaries can live up to 10 years.

- The word "parakeet" means long tail.
- Many pet parrots mimic human speech.
- The Chinese were the first to keep birds as pets.

Parakeet

Parakeets are popular cage birds. They are small to medium-sized parrots. The Australian grass parakeet (budgerigar) is one of the most common pet birds.

? Name a popular cage bird.

The Champions

Most Abundant

The red-billed queleas are the most abundant birds in the world. There are more than 1.5 billion of these birds living in the grasslands of Africa.

Longest Flyer

The Arctic tern flies the longest distance of any bird, from the Arctic north to Antarctica near the South Pole.

Fastest Flyer

The peregrine falcon is the fastest bird on earth. It can dive toward its prey at a speed of 290 to 320 kilometres (about 180 to 198 miles) per hour.

Great Walker

The emu is the bird that can walk the furthest distance. Emus are flightless birds that migrate long distances by walking. They walk at a speed of nearly 50 kilometres (30 miles) per hour, in search of water during dry seasons.

Hummingbird

The hummingbird is a small bird found in North and South America. Hummingbirds are the only birds that can hover mid-air, fly backwards, and fly vertically and horizontally. The bee hummingbird is the smallest bird in the world. It is 5 centimetres (about 2 inches) long and weighs about 2 g (0.004 pounds).

Swimmers and Divers

The penguins of Antarctica are the fastest swimmers and deepest divers. Most of them can dive to depths of over 400 metres (about 0.2 miles) and swim at speeds of up to 8 kilometres (about 5 miles) per hour. The gentoo penguin is the fastest underwater penguin. It can swim at a speed of up to 36 kilometres (about 22 miles) per hour. The emperor penguin can stay underwater for 27 minutes, which is the longest duration of all birds, during a dive.

- Bald eagles build the largest nests of any living bird; the largest nest was found in St. Petersburg, Florida, in 1963, weighing almost 2 tonnes and measuring 2.9 m wide and 6 m deep.
- Hummingbirds have the fastest heartbeats, with their hearts beating 1,263 beats per minute.

Which is the smallest bird in the world?

Endangered Birds

Many species of birds are endangered, meaning they are in danger of dying out. The lives of these birds are threatened by natural causes or by human activities, such as hunting, capturing them in order to sell them as pets, and the destruction of their natural habitat. Human beings have cleared acres of forestland everywhere on earth, leaving many birds homeless.

Whooping Crane

The whooping crane is the tallest bird in North America. It was about to become extinct in the late 1930s. However, it was saved, and today there are more than 800 whooping cranes.

Black Robin

The black robin, or Chatham Island robin, is a small, sparrow-sized bird found in the Chatham Islands of New Zealand. In 1981, this bird was on the verge of extinction. However, the bird was saved, and today, there are around 300 black robins in the Chatham Islands.

Po´ouli

The po´ouli (black-faced honeycreeper) is a small forest bird found in Hawaii. It is a critically endangered species. There are only 3 po´oulis alive, and they were last seen in 2004.

- Kakapo is the only flightless parrot in the world, but have strong legs that make them excellent climbers.
- A total of 216 birds in Australia are at risk of extinction because of the on-going deforestation for urban expansion.

California Condor

The California condor is an endangered member of the vulture family. It is the largest flying bird in North America. California condors have been saved from extinction. In 1983, there were only 22 of them left alive. However, various programmes of captive breeding helped save these birds, and today, there are over 500 California condors living in different zoos, national parks, and in the wild.

Name the vulture that has been saved from the verge of extinction.

Extinct Birds

Extinct birds are birds that have been lost forever. Over the years, many species of birds have become extinct. Extinction happens when the population of a certain species dies off faster than they are born. Extinction can be caused by humans killing or hunting or by natural causes such as climate change or natural disasters.

Great Auk

The great auk was a flightless, penguin-like bird, that were native to the Arctic and sub-Arctic regions.. The last great auk died in Iceland in 1844.

Dodo

The dodo was a large, flightless bird found in Mauritius. It had a long, hooked bill and short neck and legs. Dodos disappeared around 1690.

Moa

Moas were big birds that became extinct in the 1500s. The moas lived in the forests of New Zealand, and they were hunted by men to extinction. The giant moa was one of the largest birds ever known.

- Since 1500 A.D., 128 species of birds have become extinct.
- The last known passenger pigeon—Martha, died in the Cincinnati Zoo in Ohio, United States.

Passenger Pigeon

Passenger pigeons were common birds that were found in large numbers in North America. The number of passenger pigeons declined hugely between 1870 and 1890. They died out due to overhunting and the destruction of their habitats.

Mariana Mallard

The Mariana mallard was a large duck that lived in the islands of Guam, Tinian, Saipan, and Rota in the Mariana Archipelago in the Pacific Ocean. Wild mariana mallards were last seen on the island of Guam in 1981.

When did dodos become extinct?

Glossary

Ancestor: an organism that lived years ago, and modern forms have evolved from it

Aquatic: relating to water

Bill: stiff, projecting oral structure of certain animals

Crustaceans: an animal with a hard shell and several pairs of legs that usually lives in water

Destruction: to damage something to such an extent that it stops existing

Endangered animals: the animals that are on the verge of becoming extinct

Extinct: refers to an organism that is dead or no longer exists

Flightless: a bird or an insect naturally unable to fly

Fossil: the decayed remains of ancient plants and animals buried deep inside the earth since millions of years ago

Grassland: a large piece of land where wild grass grows

Habitat: the natural home of an organism

Hunting: pursue and kill a wild animal for sport or food

Inhabit: to reside in a particular place or environment

Mottled: marked with spots or smears of colour

Natural disasters: disasters caused by weather and climate events

Nocturnal: animals active at night

Nocturnal: to be active at night

Nourish: to supply with nutrients

Plumage: a bird's feathers collectively

Predator: an animal that naturally preys on others

Primitive: very old

Regurgitate: bring swallowed food up again to the mouth

Scavenger: an organism that feeds on the dead remains of other organisms

Talons: a claw, one belonging to a bird of prey

Threatened: on the verge of becoming endangered

Woodland: a large piece of land covered with trees

Answers

Page No. 9	Archaeopteryx
Page No. 11	Ostrich
Page No. 13	Over 240
Page No. 15	Bald eagle
Page No. 17	False
Page No. 19	Heart-shaped
Page No. 21	Waterproof
Page No. 23	18
Page No. 25	Webbed
Page No. 27	Arctic Tern
Page No. 29	Macaw
Page No. 31	Over 350
Page No. 33	Tailorbird
Page No. 35	Bee hummingbirds
Page No. 37	Parakeet
Page No. 39	Bee hummingbird
Page No. 41	California condor
Page No. 43	1690

NATURAL WORLD
PLANTS

Introduction

Plants support life on Earth. Without plants, there would be no life. They provide all living things with oxygen, food, and shelter. The first plants appeared on Earth about 450 million years ago. These plants were small and moss-like, and they evolved from algae—tiny aquatic organisms.

There are about 435,000 known species of plants. Plants grow in all corners of the world—from the deserts to the oceans and high up in the mountains. Even the cold Arctic and Antarctic regions have a few species of plants growing there.

Trees

Trees are woody plants that grow almost everywhere on Earth. There are over 73,000 different kinds of trees in the world. Some trees are tall, while others only grow a few feet.

Types of Trees

Trees are commonly divided into broadleaf, conifers and palm trees. They also include other categories like cycads, ferns, ginkgoes, etc.

Broadleaf Trees

Broadleaf trees, as the name suggests, have broad, flat leaves. They are the most common trees around the world. Most of these trees are deciduous, which means they shed their leaves seasonally, usually during autumn, and grow new leaves in the spring.

Needleleaf Trees

Needleleaf trees, as their name suggests, are trees with narrow, pointed, needle-like or thin scale-like leaves. This group includes pines, firs, spruce, yews and many more. Most needleleaf trees are evergreen, although a few of them are evergreen deciduous.

Palm Trees

Palm trees are found in the tropical regions of the world. They usually grow in coastal and dry areas. These trees have huge fan-shaped leaves. Most palm trees do not have any branches.

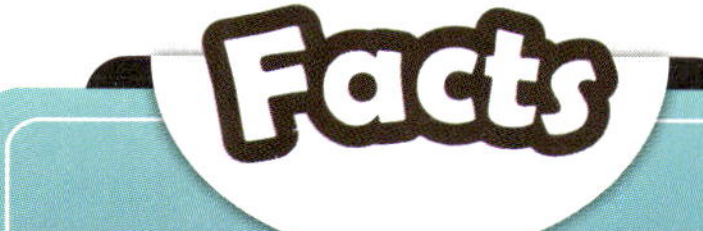

- Trees are the longest living organisms on earth.
- Large trees can absorb up to 100 gallons of water from the ground every day.

Spruce is a needleleaf tree. (True or False)

Parts of a Plant

Plants have two organ systems: the root system and the shoot system. The root system includes the parts that grow below the ground, such as roots, tubers, and rhizomes. The shoot system includes stems, leaves, flowers, fruits, and seeds.

Stem

The stem supports the plant and acts as a carrier of water and nutrients from the roots and leaves to various parts of the plant. Some plants, such as the poppy, have green stems, while others, such as oak and pine, have woody stems.

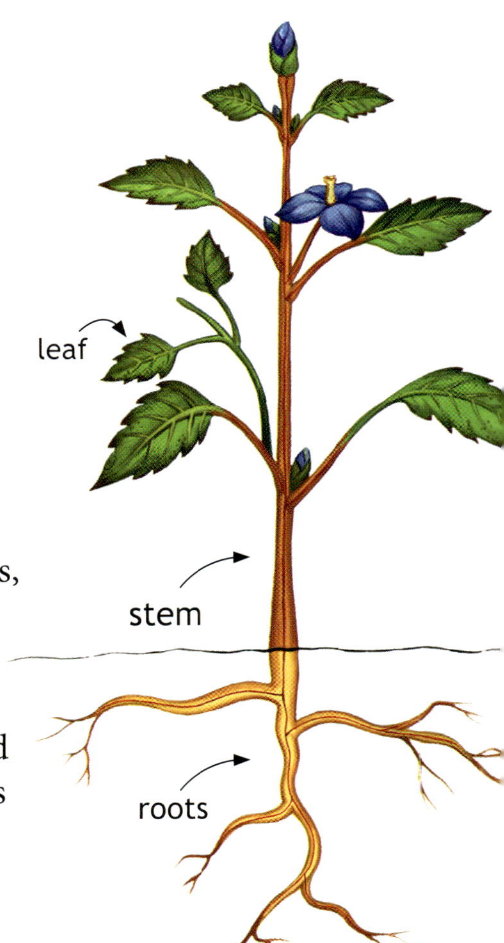

Root

Roots anchor the plant to the ground, absorb water and minerals, and act as a storehouse for extra food. Plants may have a taproot system or a fibrous root system. For example, carrots, radishes, and turnips have taproots, while weeds and grass have fibrous roots.

Leaves

Leaves are the food-manufacturing units of plants. They use sunlight, carbon dioxide, and water to make food for the plant. Leaves are of two types—simple and compound. Some plants have simple leaves, while some have compound leaves.

simple leaf

compound leaf

Flowers and Fruits

Flowers are the reproductive organs of a plant. They produce seeds that grow into new plants. The seeds of most plants are inside a soft, fleshy organ called the fruit.

- Plants with soft and bendable stems are known as herbaceous plants.
- Vegetables are different plant parts that we eat.

What are plants with bendable stems called?

Photosynthesis

Plants are autotrophs, which means they produce their own food or nutrients. They manufacture food through a natural process called photosynthesis. Plants use sunlight, water and carbon dioxide (CO2) from the atmosphere to manufacture food in the form of sugar.

Chloroplasts

Chloroplasts are large organelles present in plant cells that contain chlorophyll. The entire process of photosynthesis takes place within the chloroplasts of a plant cell.

Chlorophyll

Chlorophyll is a green-coloured pigment found in plants. In fact, the green colour of plants is due to the presence of chlorophyll. Chlorophyll helps leaves convert light energy into chemical energy during photosynthesis.

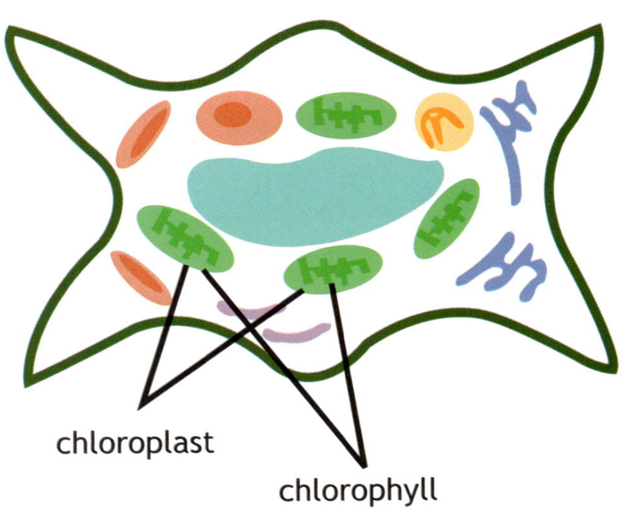

A plant cell

Products and by-products

Photosynthesis converts carbon dioxide (CO2) and water (H2O) into glucose. The process also removes carbon dioxide (CO2) from the air and releases oxygen (O2) as a by-product. The glucose and oxygen (O2) produced are essential for all living beings.

What makes plants green?

- At night, plants breathe in oxygen and release carbon dioxide.
- The Giant Water Lily has the largest leaves of any plant.

Flowering and Non-Flowering

Some plants produce flowers and seeds, which are called flowering plants. Roses, lilies, and orchids are flowering plants. Plants that do not produce flowers and seeds are called non-flowering plants. Horsetails, mosses, ferns, and pine trees are non-flowering plants.

Sedges and Horsetails

Sedges are grass-like plants. They usually grow in groups. They have a triangular stem ending in a single spike or a group of spikes on the upper section of the plant. Horsetails, on the other hand, are close relatives of ferns. They have hollow and segmented stems and some medicinal properties.

Difference

Apart from bearing flowers and seeds, flowering and non-flowering plants are different in many ways. Most flowering plants have a well-developed vascular system, whereas some non-flowering plants do not have one. A vascular system is a series of tubes and vessels that transport water and nutrients throughout the plant. Flowering plants have distinct male and female parts, whereas non-flowering plants do not have such prominent parts.

Spores

Non-flowering plants produce spores on the underside of the leaves. Spores are very tiny living organisms. Spores also play a vital role in the development of new plants.

- There are over 369,000 varieties of flowering plants in the world.
- Broccoli is both a flower and a vegetable.
- Some of the world's favourite drinks, like tea, cola, coffee, and wine, are obtained from flowering plants.

? **Is broccoli a flower or vegetable?**

Parts of a Flower

Bright and colourful, flowers are the most beautiful parts of a plant. They are the reproductive organs of flowering plants. A flower contains both the male and female reproductive parts.

Male Reproductive Parts

The male reproductive part of a flower is called the stamen. It consists of the filament and the anther. The anther produces the pollen.

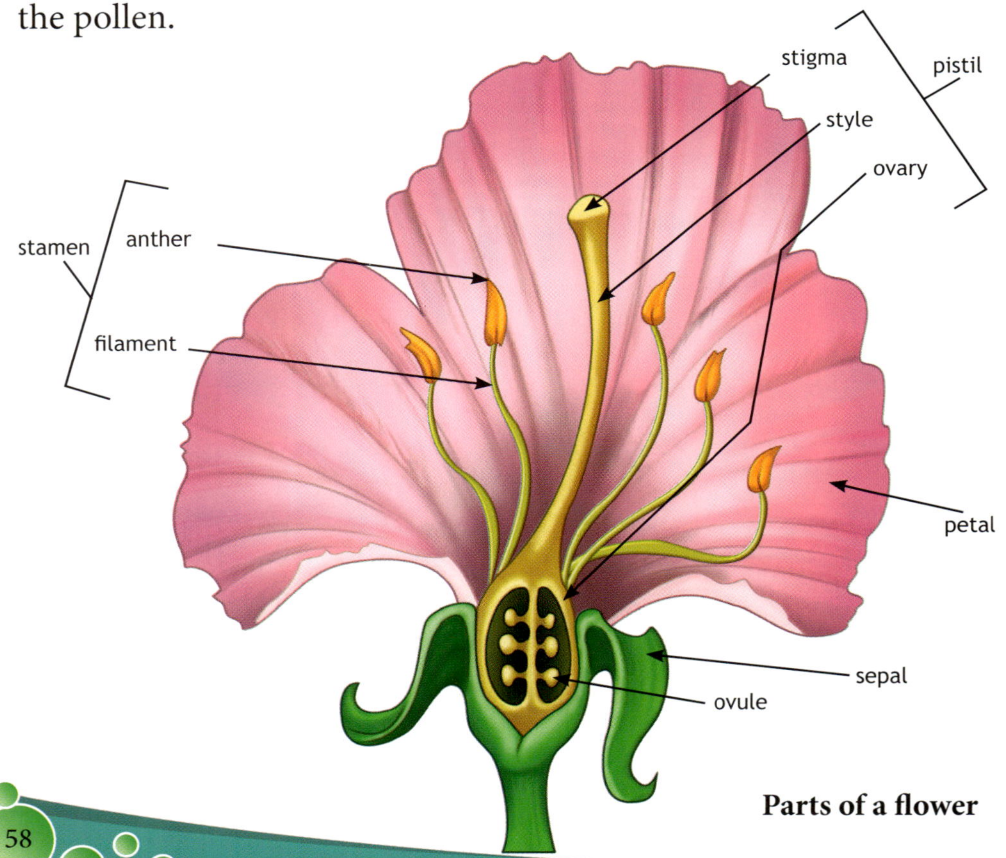

Parts of a flower

Female Reproductive Parts

The pistil is the female reproductive part of a flower. It consists of the stigma, style, ovary and ovule.

Petals

Petals are the brightly coloured outer parts of a flower. They collectively form the corolla. The petals are surrounded by a ring of small leaves known as sepals that protect the flower when it is still a bud. The sepals together are known as the calyx.

- A flower lacking one or more of the four parts found in a flower is known as an incomplete flower.
- Rafflesia arnoldii, found in the rainforests of Indonesia, is the world's largest flower.

What part of the flower produces pollen?

Pollination

Pollination is the process by which pollen grains are transferred from the male parts of a flower to the female parts. This pollen movement can occur between different flowers or happen within the same flower.

Pollen Grains

Pollen grains are tiny structures that contain the male sex cells of a plant. The grains combine with the female sex cells to produce seeds, which grow into new plants. Pollen grains are carried by wind, insects such as honeybees, other animals, or water.

Self-pollination

In self-pollination, pollen grains are transferred from the stamen to the stigma on the flowers of the same plant. Peanut plants reproduce through self-pollination.

How do insects pollinate flowers?

Flowers produce nectar. When an insect sits on a flower to sip nectar, the pollen grains stick to its body. As the insect flies from one flower to another, it transfers the pollen grains along with it.

- Hay fever is caused by pollen.
- Plants that depend on wind for pollination do not bear showy or beautiful flowers.

? **Peanut plant reproduces through ________.**

Germination

Germination is the growth and development of a new plant from a seed. The two halves of a seed contain the baby plant, called the embryo. When a seed is exposed to the right conditions, it breaks open and the baby plant emerges.

Germination requires:

- Water: Seeds are usually dry and dormant. They can germinate only when they absorb water.
- Optimum temperature: Some plants germinate at low temperatures, while others germinate when it is warm.
- Oxygen: It helps food stored in the seed break down into simpler substances.
- Light: In many plants, light initiates germination.

- The double coconut is the largest seed in the world.
- Some trees, such as the nightshade and the castor oil plant, bear poisonous seeds.

Process of Germination

Seeds are covered by a seed coat, which protects the embryo until the seed lands in a favourable environment. Seeds usually germinate in moist places where they can easily absorb a lot of water and oxygen. The water and oxygen help the embryo develop. As the embryo enlarges, the seed coat breaks open and the radicle, or main root, emerges. It grows towards the soil, and the tiny shoot grows upwards. The leaves and the side roots develop over a period of a few days.

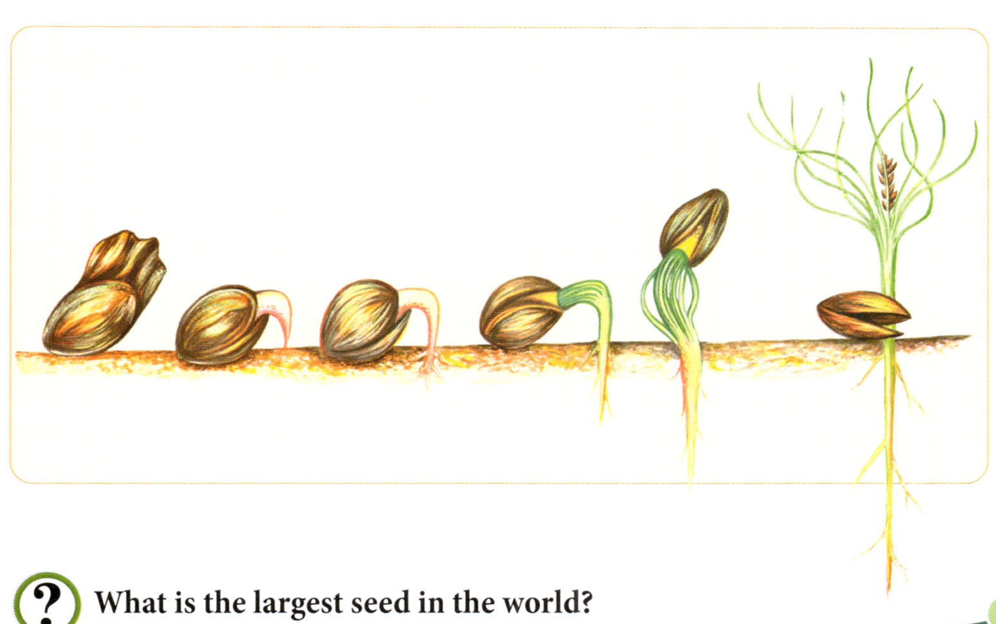

What is the largest seed in the world?

Shrub

Shrubs are short, woody plants. They usually grow up to be about 5 to 6 metres (about 16 feet) tall. They have more than one stem and several branches arise from the area near the roots. Shrubs are either deciduous or evergreen.

Deciduous or Evergreen

Some shrubs remain green throughout the year, while others shed their leaves in the autumn. Shrubs that remain green throughout the year are called evergreens, while those that shed their leaves are called deciduous shrubs.

Shrubs and Beauty

Shrubs add to the beauty of our gardens. They can be used as hedges or planted in decorative groups. Most shrubs bear bright, colourful flowers, which make our gardens very beautiful.

- The wood of holly shrubs is used to make fine chess pieces.
- Conifers such as mountain pine and juniper are shrubs.

Rhododendron

Rhododendron is a flowering evergreen shrub. It has large, shiny and leathery leaves that are red, white, pink, yellow, or lavender-coloured. Rhododendron plants bear trumpet-shaped flowers.

Michigan Holly

Michigan holly is a deciduous shrub that has soft spineless leaves. The leaves turn yellow in autumn and are shed by winter.

 **Michigan holly is an evergreen shrub. (True or False)**

Grass

Grass is a family of non-woody, flowering plants. There are almost 9,000 different species of grass. Different varieties of grass are grown as lawns, for pasture, and as food crops.

Turfgrass and Ornamental Grass

Turfgrasses such as carpet grass and Bermuda grass are used to cover playgrounds, lawns and fields. Ornamental grasses are grown in parks and gardens to add beauty to them.

Cereals

Cereals are grains of grass and a source of food for most animals and human beings. Rice, oats and several other types of corn are grass grains.

Structure of Grass

Grasses have a fibrous root system and hollow stems with swollen joints. The stems are called culms and the joints are called nodes. All grass plants have long, narrow leaves that extend out of the stem.

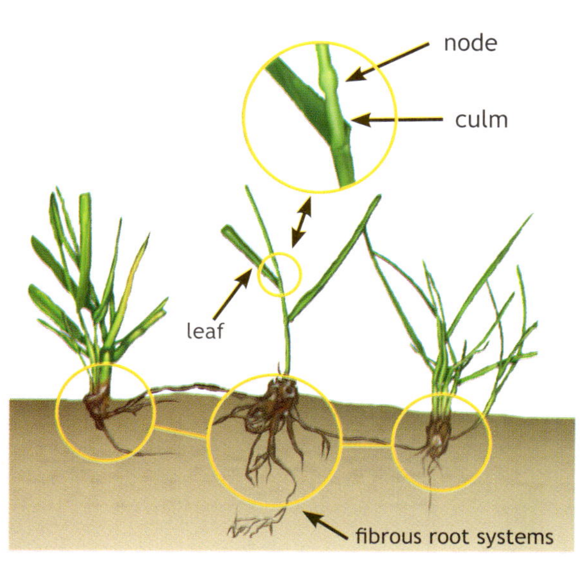

Parts of Grass

- Grasses have small flowers known as florets.
- Grass helps control soil erosion.
- Bamboo is a grass that is used to make paper.

 **What type of root system do grasses have?**

Vine

Vines are plants with long, flexible stems. They grow along the ground or climb up trees and walls, and cling to them. Vines are used for landscaping and also as ground covers in many places.

Tendrils

Tendrils are slim, spring-like stems that help vines climb and cling onto trees and other vertical surfaces by wrapping themselves around them. Grape vines and sweet pea vines climb with the help of tendrils.

Lianas and Herbaceous

Vines are divided into two categories: lianas and herbaceous. Lianas have woody stems. They grow against trees and can be hundreds of feet long. Herbaceous vines, on the other hand, have thin stems. They usually climb trees and other surfaces by twining petioles, tendrils and inflorescences.

Kudzu

Kudzu is an evergreen woody vine that grows in Japan, China and parts of Southeast Asia.

Clinging Vines

Clinging vines have aerial roots that grow from their stems or other special structures. As their name suggests, such vines cling to almost any flat surface.

What is Kudzu?

Facts

- Bougainvillaea is a woody vine that is grown as an ornamental plant almost all over the world.
- Grapes grow on deciduous, woody vines.

Conifer

Conifers are cone-bearing plants. They grow in most places around the world. There are more than 600 different species of conifers. Common conifer trees include pines, spruces, yews, cedars and redwoods.

What does a conifer look like?

Most conifers are tall, evergreen trees. They have straight trunks with horizontal branches and needle-like leaves. Some conifers have flat, triangular scale-like leaves or broad, flat strap-shaped leaves.

Cones

The cones of conifers are the reproductive organs of trees. All conifers have two types of cones: male cones and female cones. Female cones are the usual woody cones that bear the female gamete. Male cones are herbaceous. They bear the pollen.

Life Cycle of Conifers

- The pollen is carried from the male cones to the female cones by the wind.
- The pollen fertilisers the female gamete, and the seed develops.
- When the seeds are mature, the cones open up, releasing the seeds.
- The seeds usually drop to the ground and germinate when conditions are suitable.

Facts

- Conifer wood is used to make paper.
- Conifers are primitive trees that date back to the late Carboniferous Period.

? **How many species of conifers are there in the world?**

Fern

Ferns are primitive non-flowering plants that have been around for millions of years. Some of the oldest fern fossils that have been found date back to the middle Devonian period, 383-393 million years ago.

Frond

Ferns have long leaves called fronds. A frond is made up of several leaflets or pinnae, and a stipe or stem. Fronds bear spores that grow into other ferns. However, all fronds do not have spores. The ones that have spores are called fertile fronds.

Tree Fern

Tree ferns are tall, tree-like ferns that grow in New Zealand. The Black Tree Fern is the tallest and most common tree fern in New Zealand. It grows up to be 20 metres (65 feet) tall.

Facts

- There are over 12,000 species of ferns in the world.
- The King fern, found in Australia, has the longest fronds of any fern.

Where do ferns grow?

Ferns grow in warm, damp areas in forests and near water bodies. They are usually seen growing along creeks and streams or floating on the surface of ponds.

How do ferns reproduce?

Ferns reproduce from spores. The spores grow underneath fronds, inside casings called sporangia. When the spores are released from their cases, they are dispersed by the wind. If the spore lands in a suitable place, it grows into a small plant called a prothallus. The prothallus contains both male and female reproductive parts that contain the sperm and eggs. The sperm then finds an egg and the two parts fuse to grow into an adult fern.

Name the tallest tree fern of New Zealand.

Moss

Mosses are small plants that grow in damp, shady places. Moss plants do not have a stem or roots. They have small slender stalks and leaves that absorb the air and water from the atmosphere.

Moss Mats

Mosses usually grow together, forming moss mats. This helps them retain water and moisture. Growing in groups also help them stand upright, even though they do not have a stem to support them.

Facts

- Mosses lower their metabolism and become dormant during the summer season to survive the drought conditions.
- Mosses usually grow on the bark of deciduous trees.

Peat Moss

Peat moss is a kind of moss that usually grows in peat bogs. There are over 350 species of peat moss. Most of them are found in the Arctic tundra, while a few species also grow in New Zealand, Chile, Argentina and Brazil.

Peat moss grows in _________.

Aquatic Plants

Aquatic plants, or hydrophytes, grow in water. These plants have several special adaptations, such as waterproof leaves and air sacs in the stems and roots, which help them survive in water. Most aquatic plants float on water, while some of them (such as seaweed) grow underwater.

Adaptations

The leaves of most aquatic plants are covered with a waxy layer called the cuticle. The cuticle keeps the leaves waterproof. Other adaptations found in aquatic plants include flexible stems that move easily with the water current and the absence of chlorophyll and stomata from the underside of leaves.

- The water lily is a tuberous aquatic plant.
- Duckweeds are flowering aquatic plants that do not have any stems or leaves.

Seagrass

Seagrasses are marine plants that grow in shallow and sheltered coastal areas almost all over the world. They have strap-like leaves and underground stems and roots. Seagrass is a source of food for many marine animals.

Water Hyacinth

Water hyacinths are aquatic flowering plants that bear beautiful blue-purple or lilac-coloured flowers, have large elliptical or circular leaves, and have a fibrous root system that grows underwater. These plants have one of the fastest growth and reproductive rates. They pose a serious threat to many aquatic ecosystems as they tend to cover them and diminish the oxygen level of the water.

Almost all aquatic plants are covered with a waxy layer called __________.

Desert Plants

Deserts are places with extreme weather conditions. They can be very hot, dry or extremely cold. Although the climate is harsh, many plants are still able to grow and thrive in the environment.

Leaf, Stem and Root Adaptations

Desert plants have different adaptive features that help them survive in severe climatic conditions. Most desert plants have very few leaves or no leaves at all. This helps them reduce water loss. They usually have thick fleshy stems that they use to store water. They also have an extensive shallow root system to absorb surface water.

Cactus

A cactus is a desert plant with succulent stems and long fibrous roots. The leaves of cacti have been reduced to spines. Cacti are flowering plants. They bloom for a short period during the spring.

Surviving Droughts

Many desert plants shed their leaves in the dry season. This reduces the amount of water lost through transpiration. Some desert plants grow only in spring. They flower; shed their seeds; and die out before the dry season starts. The seeds remain dormant throughout the dry season and germinate in the next spring.

What is the tallest cactus in the world?

Facts

- Phreatophytes are plants that can absorb water from saturated soils.
- Ephemerals are desert plants that emerge and bloom during one season.
- The giant saguaro cactus, which grows up to a height of 24 metres (about 78 feet), is the tallest cactus in the world.

Medicinal Plants

Many chemical substances that are used in medicines are derived from plants. The first kinds of medicines that man ever used were made from the roots, leaves, stems and bark of plants. In many countries around the world, plants are still the most important source of medicine.

Herbs

Herbs are plants that are used for their medicinal and culinary properties. Medicines made from herbs are called herbal medicines. Herbal medicines are available in the form of fresh or dried plants, powders, teas, capsules and tablets.

Facts

- Eucalyptus oil, obtained from the leaves and branches of the eucalyptus tree, is an effective disinfectant and germicide.
- Aloe vera is a common plant used as a medicine for healing wounds and burns.

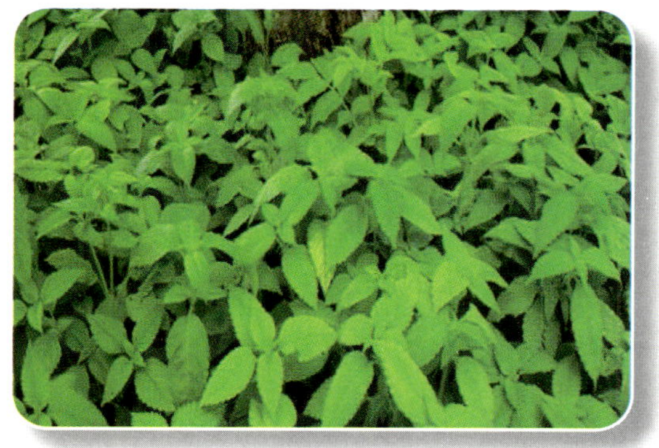

Mentha

Mentha or mint is a natural source of menthol. It is used to relieve itching and help reduce muscular pain. Mint is also used to treat sore throats and upset stomachs.

Cinchona

Quinine, the medicine used to treat malaria, is derived from the bark of the Cinchona tree. Cinchona is an evergreen tree native to South America.

Ginger

Ginger, commonly used as a spice, has many medicinal qualities. It is used to aid digestion and treat colds and headaches.

Mentha is used for treating muscular pain. (True or False)

Carnivorous Plants

Carnivorous plants are those that trap and eat living organisms. There are more than 750 different kinds of carnivorous plants. Most of these plants grow in wet conditions and in sandy soil which is usually poor in nutrients.

Venus flytrap

Venus flytraps feed on spiders, slugs, crickets, caterpillars, and flies. They have special leaves that secrete a sweet nectar to attract prey. When the prey lands on the leaf to sip the nectar, the short, stiff hair present on the leaf detects its presence, and the leaf closes down on the insect, trapping it within. The leaves reopened after about 12 hours.

Sundew

Sundews are beautiful carnivorous plants. They have tentacles with sticky gel-like substances on the tips all over their leaves. These tentacles help trap the prey. When insects fly near the leaves, they get stuck to the gel-like substance and are entangled by the tentacles.

Pitcher Plants

Pitcher plants have pitcher- or goblet-shaped leaves filled with digestive juices. When an insect sits on its leaves, it slips down into the pool and the process of digestion begins.

Facts

- Venus flytraps grow in bogs and wetlands in North and South Carolina in the United States.
- Bladderworts can trap and suck their preys in 1/50 of a second.

 **Venus flytrap is the name of a ______.**

Botanical Gardens

A botanical garden is a place where a wide variety of plants are grown for scientific and educational research. It is a garden where rare and threatened species of plants are also cultivated. Botanical gardens usually have greenhouses and herbariums and are open to the public.

Greenhouse

A greenhouse or glasshouse is a type of house made of either glass or plastic for growing plants. Plants are grown inside them to protect them from extreme cold and heat. The temperature inside the greenhouse increases when sunlight falls on it; the heat is absorbed by the plants and soil.

Kew Gardens

The Royal Botanical Gardens, or Kew Gardens, located in Kew, London, is one of the most popular botanical gardens in the world. It has more than 60,000 diverse varieties of plants. The garden's herbarium is one of the largest in the world. It has more than seven million plant specimens.

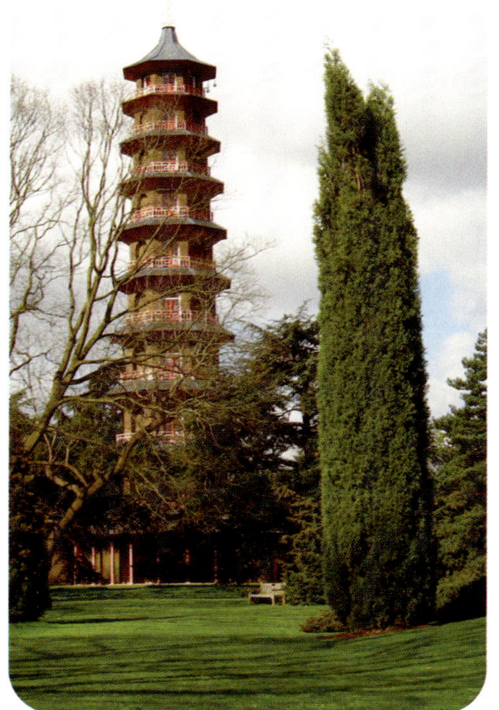

Facts

- A herbarium is a building that houses a collection of dried plants.
- An arboretum is a botanical garden where a diverse range of woody plants are cultivated.
- There are about 1,800 botanical gardens around the world.

Botanical gardens are open to public. (True or False)

Glossary

Aerial: related to air

Anchor: to hold firmly

Bog: a wetland that is always partially covered with water

Dormant: to remain inactive or in a state of sleep

Drought: a long period marked by a scarcity of precipitation leading to an extreme shortage of water

Emerge: to come out

Environment: the surroundings in which we live with all the things, such as air, water, etc., that affect us

Fossil: remains or traces of dead animals and plants

Germicide: a chemical used to kill germs

Hay fever: a type of fever caused by inhaling pollens

Inflorescence: a cluster of flowers on a stem

Metabolism: a process of producing energy from food

Nectar: a sweet liquid produced by flowers

Organelles: body parts of a cell

Pasture: land covered with small plants and grass used for grazing by animals

Petiole: leaf stalk

Plant: a plant that is used for decorative purposes in the house or elsewhere

Primitive: very old or ancient

Rhizome: a thick plant stem that grows along the ground

Specimen: an example or sample of something

Stomata: tiny pores on leaves that help in transpiration

Tropical: the warm region of earth lying between the Tropic of Cancer and the Tropic of Capricorn

Tundra: a place where trees and plants do not grow because of cold temperatures

Weed: an unwanted or uncultivated plant

Answers

Page No. 51 True

Page No. 53 Herbaceous plants

Page No. 55 Chlorophyll

Page No. 57 Both

Page No. 59 Anther

Page No. 61 Self pollination

Page No. 63 Double coconut

Page No. 65 False

Page No. 67 Fibrous root system

Page No. 69 An evergreen vine

Page No. 71 More than 600

Page No. 73 Black Tree fern

Page No. 75 Peat bogs

Page No. 77 Cuticle

Page No. 79 Giant saguaro cactus

Page No. 81 True

Page No. 83 Carnivorous plant

Page No. 85 True